Happiness

Happiness

Frederick Pollack

STORY LINE PRESS
1998

Published by Story line Press, Inc.
Three Oaks Farm
PO Box 1108
Ashland OR 97520-0052

This publication was made possible thanks in part to the generous support of
the Andrew W. Mellon Foundation, the Charles Schwab Corporation Founda-
tion, the Nicholas Roerich Museum, The Oregon Arts Commission, The San
Francisco Foundation and our individual contributors.

Page design by Paul Joseph Pope

Library of Congress Cataloging-in-Publication Data

Pollack, Frederick, b. 1946–
  Happiness / Frederick Pollack.
     p. cm
  ISBN 1-885266-58-8
  I. Title.
PS3566.04797H36   1998
811'.54—dc21

98-7890
CIP

for Phylis

Revolutionary in Heaven:
Frederick Pollack's *Happiness*

If the Left has a metaphysics — and most Leftists would tell you it absolutely does not — it would be embodied in Frederick Pollack's narrative poem, *Happiness*. Due to the kind of anomaly Stephen Hawking has described in his astrophysics, the universe has turned inside out, and those who would change the world for its own good, i.e. do away with capitalism and all its works, are in charge. Hawking himself is a character, lurking in the margins of this poem, monitoring the durability of this new condition which dates from X-day when time and space inverted. Meanwhile, there is a wall between this utopia and the world where its newleaders were mere drudges, losers, Marxists. Approach the wall and nausea overcomes you, your ears bleed. Otherwise, it looks like the Las Vegas Strip.

Frederick Pollack has explored the world of wish fulfillment previously in his epic poem, *The Adventure*. There an intellectual of the Me-decade, after committing suicide, finds himself in a three-stage afterlife, moving from a fantastic comics landscape, where all his appetites are gratified, to an increasingly more complicated society where wishes are not so easily granted, because of the desires of others. *The Adventure* is a journey through modern intellectual life, with the nameless hero enjoying audiences with the likes of Soren Kierkegaard and Gottfried Benn, and discovering just how many of his most cherished ideals can actually endure in an afterlife where they are given free rein. Written in tercets to echo the famous verses of Dante's afterworld narrative, The Adventure is a great experiment in free verse storytelling — lucid, swiftly moving, traveling between but never overflowing onto the banks of prose.

Happiness, like *The Adventure*, is in three parts, but the sections do not correspond as clearly to the development of one character's awareness of self and others. The free verse, divided into quatrains, is choppier, more intense, and the overall poem is in 32 episodic sections of different lengths. All light in *The Adventure* comes from an unfixed source on the dome that separates the underworld from the overworld. *Happiness* is more garishly lit, though with a similar division between here and there. And though our attention is focused on a first person narrator, a protagonist, if you will, even a hero, we are also engaged in the fates or interests of his cohorts, a group of enforcers who dispense rough justice and tender mercies, taking advantage of all that was not possible before the Hawking anomaly.

Here the reader may find the most difficult aspect of *Happiness*. The band of avengers we follow on its careening way through North America serves rather like Dante's devils in the *Inferno*, meting out just punishments to abusive parents and fat cats who have been caught on this side of the wall after X-day. Despite the satisfying nature of these punishments and occasional rewards (the miserable in mind and body are restored to health), the hardest thing to accept is that for the enforcers, doing justice in this fashion constitutes happiness. And yet we flock to movies in which intrepid gangs — the Mission Impossible force, for example — settle the hash of evil agents. It is clear that commandos love their work. But in this society, where by the wave of a wand, the mind can be changed as easily as the body, the problem is expressed simply and eloquently by one character: "I / know my own / thoughts were / stupid, but / I want them / back."

Nothing lasts forever. The Hawking anomaly has its end. The phenomenon of Frederick Pollack, however, ought to have its lasting beginning in *The Adventure*, a wonderful story superbly told in verse, and now *Happiness*, as disturbing as it is original. And it is originality, that sense that poetry is close to its ground of being, that we find in Frederick Pollack's epic poetry. Even at its most farfetched, it shows us the life, both real and ideal, of our era, the gods we worship, our customs and traditions, our folkways and social norms, our dreams and nightmares, all in a voice and rhythm that are as much of our time as Homer's were of his.

Mark Jarman
Nashville, Tennessee
August, 1997

So desert it would have to be, so walled . . .

— Frost

1

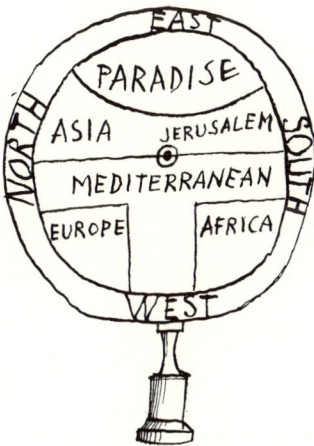

1

The Wall was
ugly. Colors
entered the mix — neon
greens, electric

pinks — lacking even the
doubtful beauty
of fractals,
but would not settle

into white
or mud. Shapes
appeared, meters,
kilometers across

and vanished. They resembled
the contents of full,
or ulcerous, rotting
stomachs

or clotted alveoles
or
bronchae. Sometimes
something like a

crash appeared,
always
head-on, immediately obscured
by fire or

metal; and sometimes
grotesque recoiling faces,
splayed
cartoon-like hands. No one

could gaze at
the Wall without
vomiting. But if (after
vomiting),

led on by
duty, you approached it,
the Wall
had no smell — rather

seemed to fight you
for air. And it made
no sound — only, your
ears bled and

hurt for hours. No one who
faced the Wall
squarely could touch it
or want to

enter and
merge with it,
but few
faced it.

It was a
cross-section. On the
far side was
the world we knew; on this side

Aidenn.

2

Hawking never called
it that; he
knew the reference
but

interpreted it narrowly.
"That was a calm
posthumous existence in a
story," he said.

"By Poe," I nodded.
— "What we have
here isn't
an afterlife," he pointed out.

"You'd like it to be,
since that would free you
from responsibility." —
"I'm not evading

responsibility — " But
he,
as ever,
mildly: "The problem with humanists

is that they assume
to understand is to metaphorize." "But isn't
physics itself a
metaphor, here?" —

I,
limply. He,
disgusted but
still polite: "Of what?"

"Of my metaphor," I
mumbled.
(I wasn't surprised
that he recognized

"Aidenn." Nothing about Hawking
surprised me,
now that he wore
good tweeds

and filled them out
and strode
from one bank of
indicators to

the next when
I visited. "There's no need,"
he said,
"for labcoats: nothing

to spill, no bureaucrats
to impress,
and the 'explosion,'
if it comes, will be

general." The famous face
was much the
same, the Earth-blue
eyes, even

the glasses; and
the appetites that
kept him
away from headquarters

most nights.)

3

Also he
never called
the Wall
a wall. "It's essential" (he

had said,
the day I threw the switch) "to see
the Anomaly
as a whole.

There is a . . .
zone, and a
boundary of sorts, but they
are non-topological.

Also non-temporal. I've heard
considerable loose talk
about
'another Arrow of Time'

'moving'
'another' direction on the
sphere of space-time; I must insist
this is nonsense. We

move no more than
the sphere does. Only,
we gather and
concentrate

certain particles
into a field —" "Why do you call it
an anomaly, when
we

created it?" I asked. "Is
that our
alibi, in case it
collapses and we're caught?"

— Rare Hawking smile. Hours
before, while he was disabled,
he had always
seemed to be smiling;

now
not. "It's also possible,"
he said
(the voice

was rusty), "that the density
of the field
increases. Then the sphere will,
so to speak,

invert.
The familiar universe
will be the anomaly, something like
a fading scar. And

we shall be nature."

4

It was, however, likelier
that the
field
would prove unsustainable and the

anomaly,
indeed, collapse. Then
the Wall, that
immense suspended shitwave

would — What?
suck us up.
No one on
the science staff

knew how quickly or slowly
that would happen. Probably
instantaneously — which
(I said) I

regretted: I'd rather
experience failure.
Moreover, no one knew
how much or whether it

would hurt. For these reasons
I reported
from the field by
radio, seldom visited

headquarters, kept up
a manic pace in
my
campaigns along

the Wall. Yet
Hawking generally ignored
risk, pain, and
my efforts. For

if the Big Balloon
in fact turned inside out,
these
would be followed by

something completely different. So after
stating my
intentions and being
patronized, I

left him
and wandered our
purloined reactor,
whose wall was

one centimeter from
the Wall. Needles
fluctuated
behind tangles

of fiber-op . . . all that extra stuff
we had stolen.
Technicians
scurried . . . I could never

talk with them. Was
glad they were on
our side, but
made eye-contact

with people manning desks
and computers:
Chomsky,
Berger, Doris Lessing, a number of

other *alte Kämpfer*.

5

And then went out to my jeep.
Rank
was nominal; sometimes I drove,
sometimes my

driver,
radioman, or
gunner. We sped from
the reactor, and

the Wall, to a north-south highway
paralleling it
two klicks east. The sky was
splendid. It was fall

or at least
had been fall on X-day; it still seemed
fall. Here and there,
high brilliant

cumulus clouds
faced the sun
like
profiles or shields

or buildings (those wave-shaped
Expressionist fancies), and gave
dimension to
the sky. The

massed subdivision
houses on the far
horizon appeared
sharp-edged; the wind

was sharp.
Our weapons
were laser-Uzis.
Our jeep

ran fast and
silently on
two small batteries.
It had appeared

when we had; these
wonders came idly,
almost
contemptuously from

headquarters. If someone
we passed raised
a weapon against us,
he soon

lowered it again,
feeling
stupid and
bored. When on rare

occasions we faced
worse resistance, I
called headquarters,
and they provided

or modified energies.

6

For example: in
those houses —
the first time
we had passed — something like

bullets
had
hit
the flocked wallpaper,

marble-patterned
mirrors,
mirrors with beer labels
or car names, lucite

chandeliers
where they were attached to
eight-foot ceilings, white or
upholstered

pianos, fake-African
carvings, fake-Empire torchieres,
purple plastic panthers, reproductions
in various media of

Durer's "Praying Hands," framed airbrushed
family portraits,
seascapes, and
Reader's Digest Condensed

Books. The fragments
didn't spatter
the living rooms and
rec rooms, but dissolved

and sifted to the
carpets.
And the people
in the houses

found they could not be
angry, but
examined their memories
of these objects, and ran

outside, not
crying but
thinking: I see how
I was misled, even

brutalized by those objects
but not
what to replace them with.
And how can I

replace them in
this house? Even the house
is tacky . . . But by then
our jeep

was gone. My
driver, Keith, didn't
approve. "People have a right
to their own tastes and

personalities."
— "That was
the point," said
my gunner,

Renata. — "How can you say that?"
Keith
started his
Woody Allen whine. — "Knock it off,

both of you," I
said. "Mister,
what I call 'taste'
is absolute. What you call 'personality'

isn't."

7

Afterwards, on
that route, we
avoided
gunplay and listened to

the radio. On
X-day, in areas
far from the Wall,
the first sign

it had gone up
was,
for young people, the difference
in radio. However far

they searched, they
couldn't find the
thump thump, the Baby baby baby,
the Yo

bitch. Instead I gave them
Arthur Klein's
first concerto, the composer
performing. A virile,

disarmingly sincere
synthesis of neoromantic and
"classically"
tone-cluster elements, this

concerto (of
more than
Busoniesque proportions) is notable
equally for the brio

of its first movement,
the unrestrained pathos
of its adagio,
the lyric inwardness

of its prolonged
conclusion. Klein hadn't
existed —
any more than

his concerto — before that day,
but I thought,
stupidly, They might enjoy this;
it's

rousing. Afterwards I played
old favorites of mine
whose feelings seemed
to represent

the moment: Sibelius, Henze. For
me it was
an emotional
debauch. (Other wavelengths

carried only
our announcement.) The young twirled
their dials;
they took off their

headphones and
stamped on them. For without the
music
that had lubricated their

lives, Being
seemed empty, and at the same time
obstructed,
gluey. "What is this shit?"

they yelled
in cars, on corners. And because
they couldn't answer
each other,

they
screamed at
each other. But when they tried
to lift their

fists or
guns, they had no strength;
betrayed by
their limbs, they felt small and

fragile, like
the old,
and began to cry, like
the old, until

I let them understand.

8

Something similar happened,
that
first day,
in schools. Mrs. Nyman

entered the room
in which (in
a sense) she taught
ninth-grade

English. It was Friday,
towards the end
of the day
and the semester

and her career. A
friend of
her late husband
had offered a

new life: office manager
for a small
brokerage.
Now more than ever

she
tried to look
fearless, as
she strode to

her desk — focusing
first on
the tears of
five-months-pregnant Seashell, the coded

profanity and hand-gestures
of
The Princess, and
the noise

of the shorter, weaker
boys, before addressing
the Males
(as the staff

called them) who sat
in back —
big,
stoned, armed, and, by

now, wholly unconscious
of her. Since he had
half-heartedly
stabbed her and served

a month's suspension, Latrobe
had been quiet,
listening only
for his beeper; while

King Satellite's
trips to
Detention and back
— paralleling

more serious
adventures — were, with
pussy, the topics
of his unceasing,

medium-loud monologue . . . (Was that a
message, a *project* of
some sort, Mrs.
Nyman

wondered — even a kind
of work? For he had
long since stopped
any attempt

at schoolwork; he knew
they would pass him
regardless . . .) But at that moment
the King saw

himself from outside. He
couldn't see where
he was seeing himself
from; he only saw

something small
and
funny. It wanted to fight
by groping Lateesha

or waving the
gun the
metal-detectors
hadn't found, but he saw

that these actions
were funny. Latrobe saw,
even more
clearly, a little puppet

with
affectations
and violence like
big jerks

on the strings. Mrs. Nyman
didn't understand their
silence. The
Seashell tried

to cry, but couldn't
get into herself
enough. "I didn't want
to be pregnant," she said

suddenly. "I didn't want
'something to hold,' any of that shit.
I just let myself
get taken over.

I was . . .
passive." — "When my momma get
high, she crazy,"
said

Latrobe. "I don't run dope
for the money — they ain't hardly
give me none.
I

like the gang 'cause . . . you don't
have to love nobody."
Their voices
croaked as if

hurt.
Everyone had something
to say, but
no one interrupted;

it was as if
they wanted
to hear. "Whoever you are,
stop doing this.

Stop it," said Mrs.
Nyman. "You're being a bully." —
"I deny that," I said. "I'm
helping you do

your job. I'm giving them
a language, a critical language,
hence a culture." She
muttered something about

"their own culture," but I said,
"You don't believe
that nonsense, do you?"
— "No, but I

do believe in
their freedom. In
freedom generally.
Don't you?" she demanded.

"No," I said.

9

We drove south.
Our
first stop
was a hospital. Formerly

I had hated
these places; now
more so.
Renata

stayed with the
jeep and
Keith; she refused,
she said,

the nurturant role. So I took
Evan, my
radioman;
he was adept

at monitoring
the Glove. We
went into
the chapel

off the main
lobby. Evan
applied contacts, tested
cables between

my hand and
the console while I
fidgeted. The
p.a.

frantically paged
the Director.
We
had met. He had done wonders

moving
new patients in
since our last visit, but
again brought

a squad
of doctors and nurses and
administrators. "These
people are clutter,"

I growled; Evan made them
fall in and shut
up.
("Pretend it's rounds,"

he said.) We went
first to
the Burn Unit. I placed
fingers on

whatever flesh
was left — a square inch
of cheek
or foot — and drew them

over the
wet mess. "Oh . . . it's
cool," they said,
if they were conscious. ("It's

not sterilized,"
said a new
intern. — "It's not *matter*,"
said Evan.) By

the end,
usually, they were
asleep with
their new

nerves. The stroking motion
calmed me, steadied
my hand. We went
upstairs. In

the chaotic
intake wards, they
had a schizophrenic. Evan attached
the visor; I

saw the subcortical
lesions, the
dendrites pointing
every which

way. I smoothed
the lesions, lined up
the cells,
rearranged

veins. She looked amazed, but
said nothing;
she wouldn't talk for
a while. Evan registered

a power surge
blanketing
Aidenn; we waited a
moment. (Really

the Glove was
superfluous, but it made things
psychologically
easier.) Now I

moved fast. From
the next head
(the
nurses crying

and crossing themselves
behind me), I drew
an amazingly large and hard
greenish

tumor, ligated
blood vessels,
relieved
swelling. Live flesh felt

like nothing.
(I had tried,
predictably, to
push into

a corpse, but it was
clammy,
painful, like −
I imagined − the Wall.) I

reached into
lungs that were barely
there,
pulled out big

gobs of the crap and
tossed it at
a basin. I stretched
good

tissue, saw it
take. When he
had air, he
looked at me,

blubbering: "I'll never do it
again. I'll never smoke again." — "You're
fucking
right,"

I yelled. ("He'll lose
the craving?" the Director
stammered. Evan
shrugged.) I hated

wasting time on
him, for there was
all that intestinal cancer
in the next three

beds. This I
just grabbed and
flung at
the floor, livid

dense lumps of
shit. I was
crying now;
I believe

everyone was, including
that patient
who waits forever, incurable
and inconsolable.

mors stupevit

10

And AIDS, of course,
and whatever Hawking had
had, and
even such things

as acne . . . millions of teenagers
still roamed the Zone,
wonderingly
touching their faces . . . A

Yale Med
researcher (he was
an early
plotter) had told me

it was theoretically possible
— given enough,
and sufficiently precise,
power — to

sort of *reason*
with a virus ("tell it, If you flourish
your host will die,
as will

you; isn't it better
to remain unborn?"). And
so we
reasoned,

with the help of
a ray from
headquarters. On the way
to our next stop, we discussed

what that stop was
for. Not a "trial"
or a "clinic," though it had aspects
of both. Nor

could one accept
"browsing" (Renata's
suggestion), though the place
was a

shopping center. "A lynching,"
said Keith
glumly. "An amnesty" –
Evan,

brightly. We parked.
The crowd was
smaller than last time.
Cops cleared a space. Renata

detached the M-60
and slung it
across her back, as
we filed

into a storefront
empty all the "recession"
years. First up
was a girl

who in pallor and profile resembled
Mrs. Punch.
"I hate my face,"
she said.

"And my skin.
 I want to change them." –
"Well, you should," from
Renata. – "Did you ask

your parents how they
felt?" asked Keith.
 – "Do I have to?"
the girl

asked, alarmed.
"Absolutely not,"
I said. I used
the Wand for

this one; it attached to
the same console
as the Glove. I
wore down

the bulbous chin, reduced
the nose, toned up breasts,
belly and
thighs (I used

the visor; no one had to
undress),
tautened and tanned
the skin, and changed

a few chromosomes
so my work might
survive. She
took five minutes,

a paraplegic ten,
then there were twenty or thirty
"blobs" (− Renata,
impatient):

clients who had
a doctor's certificate
of incurability but
shouldn't have. Abortions.

Anorexia. Back
pain. Keith checked
documents; a
vain task that

kept him out
of trouble. Meanwhile Evan patrolled,
incognito, the parking lot,
past the crowd

of cured people, who
stood
testing new
limbs and

voices, or watched themselves
in shopwindows and
tried to decide
what to do; and past the shoppers

in the new
moneyless
stores. Everyone had
taken, by

this point, a VCR,
a computer, new
microwave,
whatever was

needed; it was unclear
whether more would be
forthcoming, but there were adequate
clothes and

food. Evan
listened,
recorded, quietly
led people to

us, and when
the sick were healed, we
started on
the cruel. A kid accused

his stepfather of
abuse. We checked, via
a gadget
even Hawking had shown

some interest in: it showed
a specific subject's
past. The monitor
was small

but what appeared
was evil. We contacted the swine.
"This is a
Special Action Squad

of the Provisional Revolutionary Government.
We are called
the Avengers of Wrong.
Your

stepson has drawn
our attention to
certain crimes. It's
only fitting

your punishment should be
at his hands." This part
was voluntary, but the kid
was game:

strictures about trauma
and love of the
oppressor didn't
apply

in Aidenn. The Glove
barely fit his
hand. He
tapped once,

then when he saw
the result, swung,
swung again . . .
eyeballs,

teeth, torn-off
limbs, bits
of skull,
brains finally; and pleading,

screaming, silence. We gave him
a voucher for transport,
space in a communal
flat, and therapy

at the new in-Zone apartment
complex (the
same to which
we had referred

Ms. Punch). "Where is he?"
the
kid asked,
disoriented. — "When people

die here,
they return behind
the Wall," I said.
"They're alive there. That's why

the body
disappeared." — "But
what if your experiment
fails?

I'll go back
and he'll be waiting." —
Renata and I
glanced at each other. It's

impossible
to keep anything
secret. "As near as we
can figure, time

is different there,"
I said. "He may be
two hundred years ahead or twenty thousand
back. Neanderthals may get him

or more advanced
people. In any case,
you'll never see him."
He

left, impassive. We
started on misogynists;
or would have, but
a client who — next in

line at the door —
had watched
the proceedings, became
upset. "What you're doing

is *horrible*! It isn't right
for a kid to, it isn't
justice — " I would have
slapped her, but

Renata
chilled her with
some fascinating remark.
This woman

had come, we gathered, to
rip the testicles
off some pimp, but
now fled

unavenged. The next client
asked why we couldn't
eliminate sexism
at one blow, with a

ray. "It's too complex
a phenomenon," said Renata.
"We can inhibit
behaviors — female

circumcision, the veil,
rape — but actual sanctions
must be made
on a case-by-case

basis." By now
it was time for
lunch. I
left the M-60

with Evan, and Evan with
the silent, stricken,
Keith.
Renata went

to look, she said, for
some new
boots.
I grabbed a hamburger

and explored. It was
one of those places
between other places. The
shopping center

and a multi-island
diesel station shared
a vast asphalt
surface with

a few
cheap
apartment buildings; these turned
their backs

on a desert. I wandered
eating
under the irremediable sun, then
entered an apartment

building.
Decades had peeled
plaster, warped
doors, darkened almost every

ceiling panel.
The stairs
were sunlit. From
above, sounds

of partying: disco
(somehow),
laughter of women
preparing to be unrestrained.

That was the third floor.
I walked the first, then
the second,
on which a beautiful

woman stood
dramatically backlit before
a door.
Her hands

were fists. I
would have approached her,
asked her why, but
another door

opened. "You're the officer
from that jeep," said an
old man.
— "Yes."

— "Come in." The colorless
walls were covered
with prior attempts
to defeat

the Wall: posters of amazing
age and
enthusiasm, worn Mexican rugs,
books. Why he had

gone to ground here,
how he had
survived, remained mysteries. He
pressed my hands

between his trembling
hands, forced tea
upon me.
"My wife is ill.

In a moment, you'll
go in and wake her.
She'll be so happy. But first
I must ask you,

how long . . . ?"
"We're not
sure," I said. "It will either
collapse or

suddenly
jump to an infinitely
higher stage." — "And it was really
Hawking who was

responsible?" —
"Mostly people like us," I said
sharply,
but he

went on: "I'd be happy
if it could stay at
this level. I
go down to

the shops, and
— days I
can drive —
to the towns

around here; I see
the changes. They're learning.
It's
as we always predicted:

the instincts for workmanship,
meaning, gregariousness replace
profit and
inertia;

people make pastries
and clothes and art for
each other and
for praise. Your

cadres have been
excellent — they explain
what's available,
what's needed, and

where the work is."
He paused. "I come home and
tell her. She
can't wait to

see. They gave me medicine
for her, they
said it
would help her

through this crisis, but
then I should take her
back to the hospital. The doctors say
not even you can

save her, but that's just
jealousy . . . fetishized
professionalism, an unconstructive attitude."
He

frowned significantly
at me; I told him
we'd check it out.
He was

thoughtful, still
happy; I didn't want
to rush him. "You know,
she was the one

who read up on
Marxism and psychoanalysis,
Marxism and religion and
so on . . . I was too

demoralized.
We were accustomed
to seeing everything
discredited; it seemed right

that we should be old
now. The
completeness of our defeat
was a token

of the completeness, someday,
of our vindication. Or
so we told
ourselves. But it was hard: the

rotting city, those
feral children . . . it was the
'barbarism' Marx spoke of.
And now

we're not afraid.
We can have
a new life. It makes sense
that you appeared

at this time." I told him
something square-jawed and
heartening,
and went in

to see the wife. The
bedroom was tiny,
dark behind worn
drapes, and filled with

medicine smells. As my eyes
adjusted, I
saw the medicine bottles,
oxygen canisters, the rank

untenanted bed.

11

I had appointments,
so our afternoon
clinic ("assize?" —
Evan) was

brief. On the road
again, Renata condemned
the failures of the Revolution:
shortages of

boots and moisturizer. "It's
not a revolution.
It's a coup,"
announced

Keith, who was savagely
driving. (Two things I
knew about Keith
were that he wouldn't

endanger himself and
couldn't endanger us.) I
considered the point,
broadly

agreed. Evan
summarized what had occurred
while Renata and I were at
lunch; I phoned in

a report.
The radio honored
British Composers of the
Thatcher Era and

Giacinto Scelsi.
A plausibly synthesized
Bernstein
explained them. That was

AM.
FM was mostly
news. We settled
on jazz. A

drive-in appeared,
kilometers
ahead, its pavement
cracked but its screen

busy. This was the film
that had been playing
everywhere since X-day,
and which,

I confess, I
seldom followed.
One of headquarters'
more recondite

efforts, it careened unnervingly
between the stylizations
of art and
the longueurs

of realtime. It was as if
Hollywood itself
writhed in
purgatory, trying to awaken or

die. A key-punch operator
returned to her shared
apartment, projecting neither
fulfillment nor

apathy, and made
pasta. A hundred black
youths were shot
in a prolonged

jumpcut by other black
youths. Through rusted
speakers, violin music swelled,
turned in

on itself, became
sardonic.
"It's Wagner's dream
of an unending

melody," I said, as
the screen loomed and
passed
on its windswept

plain. "Or Flaubert:
a style that
cuts into life
at any intersection point, leaves at

any point, and creates
a rounded work of art."
— Keith: "That
makes it all right, of

course, to
expropriate
the movie screens."
— Renata: "Something I've never

understood, chief,
is
why Keith is in
the squad. He's

a political and moral
conservative, he hates
us, and
there are other drivers. What's

the point?" — I: "People like Keith
engineered and enjoyed
our impotence.
Now I rather enjoy

his impotence."

2

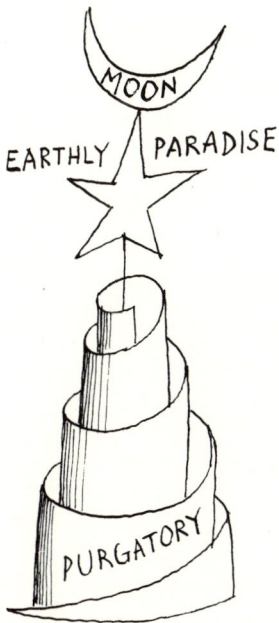

12

The restaurant
was within sight
of the Wall.
People

came here to
show courage
or defiance
or various sorts of

nostalgia, or
to do
penance. At
the bar

amid second-hand
air, one could see
former
fundamentalists,

anti-abortionists,
crude
racists — crude enough
to be changed by

a bit of
broadcast
logic. Cultists,
antisemites; on

X-day, we
had made them see
themselves through our eyes,
had made them think

our understanding of
their thoughts. Now
they
dipped their greasy fries

into a ketchup
puddle-mountain
or stared into
their drinks. Few

talked; women sat
in an absolute
gloomy
safety. Non-drinkers

could get well and truly
buzzed here;
alcoholics
found their scotch becoming

a bitter water.

13

The televisions — one
over the bar,
one in a corner — showed
the War Crimes Trial.

It was what
was on. Among
the judges, the
stern-faced

female Princeton ecologist
had been replaced by
a sad-eyed
male, and

the old,
sour
Left scholar (he had
taught and taught

but never liked
deconstruction, so wasn't
trusted;
we trusted him) drooped

visibly. I wondered if
he'd make it. The attractive
black female
defense co-counsel

(a good move,
I'd
thought) had given way
to someone more austere, but

otherwise
the two sides
had not changed. It was (as
Evan said) often hard to say

why someone was on
the stand and not
the panel
or on the panel

and not accused — "more like a mutual
plea-bargain than a
trial";
even our

star, the famous
consumer advocate, looked
sick between questions
and the scientists

had a propensity for
johnny-breaks.
I didn't recognize
the witness

and the control room
was slow with
captions. Wide,
sinless brow and

eyes; ex-
jock: one
would have expected
denial, amazed and

outraged protestations, but
they were not
his tactic. "Of course we knew
about displacement.

It wasn't our concern."
— "Something like
half the population migrated
into a region

ten miles square," said the
prosecutor. "These people had
fed themselves, but
within a year were importing

80% of their food."
— "It wasn't our concern,"
said the
witness. "Our concern

was to establish
a viable urban
bourgeoisie and stable
currency."

"And to increase
exports," said a judge.
– "Correct." – "Whose concern
was it, the hunger, social

breakdown,
all those problems?"
– "You may not
believe me, but I often

asked myself that.
Though in the context
of my work, and
that of my agency, it was a metaphysical

question. It had no answer." – "And
what answer
does it have now?" asked
a judge. – "It

still has no answer."

14.

The place had
a decent
minestrone, which I ordered.
Evan and Keith ordered

burgers,
Renata a *salade
niçoise*, and we all wanted
drinks. So

I missed the
swearing-in of
the next witness. From
the rustling

in the courtroom (we
had commandeered
McCormick Place in
Chicago) I gathered

that the unassuming,
middle-aged white
male facing the judges
was someone

big.
(We tried them
as we caught them, whoever was
in the Zone

on X-day, in the order
our gangs flushed
them out. So the Trial
was not,

unfortunately, a narrative;
at
best, disordered evidence
for a hundred separate decisions

that would define the entire future of
the species —
unless
failure, or

Hawking's apocalypse, forbade.)
The
regular prosecutor
graciously yielded

the floor to
Ruth Feinberg,
our
heaviest former

activist. But her questions
concerned figures,
dates,
names of

executives and
corporations, and I gazed
through dusty
Venetian blinds at

the Wall. Not
sickening
at this distance, or dramatic, it
was merely

gray; and the warehouses,
rusting
train tracks, closed
factories between us

were brown. I had
always, somehow, liked
neighborhoods like this, where
only cats

and the homeless lived. "Once this
deal was complete,"
Ruth
Feinberg was asking, "you were

guaranteed a percentage
of any future expansion —
even if
one of your conglomerates

was sold." — "As I've
stated, Ms.
Feinberg, it wasn't
I who was guaranteed

anything, but
the Trust."
— "You also stated,
Mr. Tolman, that

during your adult
life, you've been active
in all
decisions of the Trust. Otherwise,

as you put it, we'd
be talking to bankers."
— "That's
so," said Tolman, with

the air of
someone glad to
abandon a pretence. "To anticipate
your questions, Ms.

Feinberg," he
went on, waving away
lawyers, "I knew about
the Asian girls

who were drawn from their
villages, lived in barracks, and
lost their
eyes, lungs, and

chances of marriage
while assembling
microchips. I knew about
their sisters

who serviced tourists
and my operatives,
and even me
once or twice. I knew about

the American workers
who lost their
jobs and
benefits, drank heavily

etc. I don't think I
bear any responsibility
for these people, but you think
I do, and you —

inscrutably and temporarily —
prevail. Nor do I feel
that any other system
would treat them

better, or that their anguish
is of any ultimate importance."
— "You
make my task easier," said

Ruth Feinberg
after remarkably little
pause. "On X-day
you were worth

twelve billion dollars. What did you do
with all that?"
— "I
bought art, Ms. Feinberg,

and not as
an investment; I
despise the contemporary painters
who court us. Also

I supported
basic research — the kind that
otherwise finds
few backers. The

'anthropic principle'
debate was financed
by my funds, and I feel
some slight

connection to it . . .
Evenings I stood
on a balcony, looked
across lawns,

a creek,
trees, and considered that
I was what
everything

was for."

15

I tuned out
after that —
watched
during the afternoon

between bits of
drinking,
talking, waiting for
my appointments

to arrive and
listening to Renata bitch
about her *salade
niçoise*

("I could've told you,"
I said). No one after
Tolman was
as interesting as

he, or as amusing
as the judges: the liberals
uncomfortable with our
methods

but pretending
to be caught in
a machine; the radicals
unclear on

the concept, but thinking If
not now,
when?; the scientists
a little awkward

invoking
values, the scholars
subject to vast mood
swings on the question

of action, the few
lawyers
we had let in
quite

lost. In the field,
one did not suffer
their
ambivalence. On

the stand,
a cult leader
wasted an hour
pretending to be holier

than the
judges. (He wasn't
LaRouche, Erhard,
Miscavige, Moon: they were safe

on
the other side. I
would have liked
to get them.) Next

came a
bureaucrat
who had authorized
the pollution

of aquifers; an apologist
professor; a
chief of the
anti-abortionists (his

former followers in
the place,
watching, tensed
and

yearned towards him:
would he be
irradiated with
knowledge and redeemed,

like them?
No . . . "It doesn't
work with everyone":
Renata, our

expert,
interrupted herself to
tell them. "You
have to have

some brains." − "Also,
if one's *done* something,
one
has to be punished,"

smiled Evan).
The accused
claimed ignorance,
necessity,

obedience, that there had
been no crime or
was no law,
and were

condemned. What
followed,
unfortunately, was
never broadcast:

we
(people like
me) took them out
behind McCormick Place,

shot them, sent them home.

16

The first of my
two appointments arrived
on time.
She wore

an earth-colored,
many-textured
dress and
shawl, with

not too much
clumsy
jewelry, distinctive earrings,
boots.

The face was
intelligent and
calm,
the unreconstructed

fiftyish body comfortable.
Renata
executed a rapid
role-model survey; Evan

ran through a mental
checklist of non-sexist
lines.
"Helen Lawton,

Arts Administrator," she
said,
shaking everyone's
hand. "I was hoping

to talk to Hawking,
or Doris or *someone* at
headquarters . . . " "You'd have been
disappointed,"

I
said. "So much of
the effort there, even on
the part of

non-scientists, is dedicated
to Stephen's
ultimate
hopes, that neither

he nor anyone else
has the time
(the
interest, really) for practical organizing,

educational
reform, the medical program, or,
in your case,
art. We, however,

are interested." —
"'We' meaning
you, Captain,"
she

half-asked,
smiling at
the others, as if she wished,
for some reason, to

separate them
from me. I glanced
at them — even Keith seemed
captivated by her — and started to say

how rank was
nominal,
how we were
a team; then snarled, "Well,

I, then.
I.
Everyone had his
own reason

for joining the Revolution. You
know that thing
of Nietzsche's, that this
world can only be

justified as
an aesthetic phenomenon;
I see the Revolution
as an extension

of that."

17

"I had hoped,"
she said,
evading my
remark, "that

after the Wall
went up and there was
some
protection, the creativity

of ordinary people
would appear
from under the rubble
of media.

I worked
first — 'I' meaning
my team of
psychologists, teachers,

curators — with those people
to whom you have given a
new life,
new

bodies. I thought that they,
whose experience has been
so strange, could
initiate new

forms, but —
more important —
communicate the possibility
of a new

emotion, a change of heart."
"I wanted that
also," I said
gently.

"So
you followed us."
She nodded:
"To all those

clinics of yours [Evan: "potlatches?"]
around the Zone.
The results are
mixed. It's

impossible to separate
art and therapy in
this case . . .
Mostly they

write or paint
cliched, schematic
personal records, then
drop out,

saying they just want to
get on with their lives." ("No one can
'get on with his life'
now," said Evan.

"Life will be either
heroic or
nothing." I told him
to shut up.) "Or"

she continued, "they
beg their husbands,
parents, etc. to
take them back,

forgive them — much the way
many of them
try to recreate their
old

pointless jobs or
pay cash. The most vital
express themselves through orgies
and mayhem." "What do you think

about the parks," asked
Keith
suddenly. "His
[meaning my]

sculpture gardens." (He was referring
to the recumbent
forms of
drug addicts

who had died before
our ray could
reach them, and
the twisted

standing figures of
dealers . . . both appeared
to be made of
bronze, both were indestructible

but only the dealers
felt pain.) "I've hardly had
time for
walks —"

she said. ("My idea,"
I
said modestly. — "And
very typical," said

Keith. – "Better a
lawn ornament here than
a live junkie
there," I said,

smiling him to
silence.) Helen
Lawton pressed grimly
on: "Thereafter, I

tried to work with
the young. Those you have changed
are only interested in some
forthcoming

apocalyptic event, which
all their poems,
dances, etc. celebrate.
The others

want only their MTV
back. They
remain determinedly
illiterate, and

would kill you
if they could." – I: "I know.
They can't."
(Evan: "Early on,

as a
joke, we distributed
a couple of million
combs and little

squares of
wax paper, so they can still
make noise. And we have nothing against
jug bands." "Or vicious

humor," said Keith,
looking to
her for support, but she
wanted something.) "I

decided then,
reluctantly," she said, "to
emphasize established
talents and rely,

like any
liberal, on the trickle-down effect . . .
We contacted
composers, playwrights,

etc. and suggested
themes: hope.
The Revolution.
Redemption. We control

the museums, and after *that* —"
(she nodded at
the War Crimes Trial)
"ends,

I've been assured
we'll have access
to television." ("It'll be like
the old,

pre-cable PBS," said Renata,
delighted.
"Somewhat more leftish.") — "If
that's decided,

fine, but what do you want
from me?" I asked.
— She:
"An end to interference."

1:
"When have I ever
interfered?" — She
slowly and

clearly enunciated
some names, ending with
that of the poet
Joanna Mond. "Joanna Mond

sucked," said Renata. Grief and
outrage
contended for Helen's
face. "She was

a friend," she said. "She was
working on
a new
long poem. A revolutionary

poem. She
consulted with me
about it. She
compared the Wall

to the soil around
her dead grandmother's
grave, and your miracles
to childhood

dreams. A
chronicle of
X-day was
marvelously imbricated with

early memories that were
the major subject.
I was there
when you — not

this squad,
another – broke in, dragged her into
her garden, yelled
'In the name of modernism,

fire' and shot her." Evan
guffawed: "I remember that." –
"I don't,"
I said. "I'm sorry, I

can't keep track . . . " "It is taking
all my courage
to talk with you," said
Helen.

"Please don't distance me
with nihilistic wit." – I: "No,
really, I
can't keep track

of every idiot we
relocate.
You see,
we are not dreams.

We are nightmares
trying to become dreams." "What sort of art
do you want?" she
demanded. "A histrionic festival,"

I said.
"Unanimity.
Vast Stalinist processions, but without
lying." She stared at me,

appalled. "But
that's impossible – the form itself is
a lie." I shrugged:
"Short of that,

it scarcely matters."

18

After she
left, we
(Evan and —
I'm afraid — I)

started kidding Renata
about her. I:
"An impressive figure."
She:

"You thought so?"
Evan: "*I* did.
Mature, responsible,
respected — a

role model." "For you, maybe,"
said
Renata. — "Honestly,
why didn't you like her?"

I
asked. Renata: "She let us
give her the business
about that poetess. I wouldn't have,

for any reason." She
took a long sip
of her drink. "Also, she was
too much not

my mother." — "You were
born near here,
weren't you," I said.
— "I didn't know that,"

said Evan.
Renata: "No reason
you should.
I joined

the Revolution late." I
smiled:
"You joined
on X-day." She

nodded: "I lived in
one of those houses
you still see
between the closed

factories, the
piles of
crushed
cars, and you're amazed

that white people
live there. When the.
Wall went up,
I was just leaving

a hole-in-the-wall
book graveyard that
survived somehow
in that

neighborhood. It was where
I hung out; the
owner and I
were both ugly,

fat,
pathologically
shy. Sometimes if I liked
something long enough, he'd

give me it —
I couldn't
afford books. I only read
science fiction,

Stephen King;
that day he
gave me some
stories by H.P. Lovecraft, my

favorite. I
thought
it would be a good day
if I could get

home without
meeting the gangs
from my school. And if I
ran into

Cindy
Milligan (she was the
blonde
senior I wanted

to be), that would be heaven —
although she wouldn't
see me. And it was all
mixed up with Lovecraft:

I
knew he was
crude, but
I imagined a kind

of horror-novel
politics: vast
mouths from
space that would eat

people. Mysterious
unhuman
sages who couldn't
be killed —" "What did you imagine

for yourself?"
asked
Keith, interestingly. Renata,
strangely: "*I would ride*

with the mocking and friendly ghouls
on the night wind . . . I was very
sad and
lonely, you see. Then the wind started

and the electrical storm
that came with the
displacement
of air. I

held on to my
bag, my
book, and a lamppost and thought:
I would not tolerate

my mother any more,
the forced confessions,
midnight
masses.

The hysteria.
Or my creepy,
quasi-employed father, who controlled
only me in

the world. I
know I was
facing
the Wall — I was

two blocks away — but I don't
remember;
all I remember is
deciding: I wouldn't be

fat any more — I'd be
a knockout,
in fact. I wouldn't
be timid . . . I'd be

about
24 (I was tired of
adolescence)
and considerably

brighter.
And I wouldn't
be poor. I remember thinking:
what was happening

was power,
and power
cures. Yet I think,
now, that all those

years of escapism
helped:
generosity
seemed more attractive

than what I'd had in mind.
So I imagined
something for everyone . . .
otherwise the Revolution

might have been different." Keith
turned and
for the first time
asked

me something: "She's
mad, isn't she?"
I chuckled:
"She is my beloved daughter

in whom I am well pleased."

19

"I'm prepared to accept,"
said
Evan, "that
someone who

had nothing,
initially, to
do with our enterprise
should prove adept

at its more
esoteric
aspect. My own story
makes a related

point. Consider two men.
The first
was a punk
pulling in the big bucks

on Wall Street. His firm,
once
reputable, had been raised
by the fast tide of

the preceding period,
but stayed afloat
because it never quite broke
the law (though laws so lax

invite — don't you
think? —
breakage)
. . . In one month

he turned over properties
equal to Tolman's entire
fortune; Tolman was a client.
Now this

broker
worked hours
comparable to a hospital
intern's, but

would then spend
weeks (well,
days) water-skiing. He
reflected

his firm's
culture, refused nose candy, other
risks.
Sex was a series

of friendly takeovers
preceded by the paperwork of
tests.
Sometimes allergies

bothered him, and
a dislike of touching
public
surfaces. Still,

he rose;
some years
passed.
Parents died.

He moved
twice.
Every so often, he
had a non-power

lunch with a senior partner
of a law firm involved
with his firm. Now this man
(my

second character) was dying,
slowly and
not entirely painlessly, of
some rare but

traditional
thing. It left him mobile,
lucid,
a major

shareholder; he was only
dying. He was an embarrassment,
therefore, but —
like some

tokens or
second sons — an embarrassment
his firm couldn't
discard. And when that happens

a kind of spirituality
ensues: a
non-cash motive
everyone sees and

respects. The punk won
brownie points
for having
lunch with him. And the lawyer

seemed to like
him —
or at least
the role of mentor. He spoke of

Street personalities,
the whims of
bonds.
Yet over time

there was a change:
not only
the more frequent
pill-taking, distant

looks; he
began to disparage
the Street.
'There was a time

I still believed —
when
production and
decent

jobs came out
of it, even as
byproducts.
But now . . . '

— 'Now?' —
The lawyer
shrugged: 'You're a buccaneer,
I'm an old

servant of pirates. Do you know
there were people like us
in the first slave
ports: factotums,

agents of
houses with worldwide
interests; they drank their rum
and chewed their kif while

the slaves cried.' 'They
would have been stupid
not to,' said
the broker.

'Why so?' asked
the lawyer. — 'No alternative,'
said the
broker, 'at that stage of history.'

'And at ours?'
asked the laywer.
Then they talked,
rather more often, about

what 'an alternative'
might be.
The senior partner
was fighting a

double
deadline, pleading
with doctors and
the underground for

time, but the kid
couldn't know that.
Several
weeks passed before the broker

said 'Yes, I'm incredibly
bored —
with the rationalizations, mindless
cynicism consorting

with brainwashed gung-ho, the . . .
abêtissement? But
what are you offering?
Religion?" — and

another week
before the lawyer,
who, by
now, only

whispered, mentioned
the name Hawking.
You
remember the

last great
infusion of funds,
which paid for the
specialists

who created diversions while
we seized the reactor? The
young broker
transferred

that money, by
a variety of creative
means. He experienced
an amazing mix of

guilt,
fear and anticipation in
the months before X-day." —
"Which one

were you?" asked Keith.

20

And receiving no
answer, stared
at
bits of

pretzels
on
the table, moved
his glass in

a beer-ring . . . "Doesn't
matter," Keith mumbled.
"Either
way. Treason comes easy

when you're educated.
Since
X-day, a
voice in my head

has been trying to
educate
me. I haven't been happy
since X-day.

Wrong.
I haven't been happy
since my wife
left. She was an

unregulated woman, but
she kept
the kids.
That's O.K. — they're

safe from
you.
She wasn't
much of a Christian, but

she'll give them a
Christian education. –
I don't
really care. When I

say that, I'm
just
trying to hurt
you. As if

you couldn't get them,
because they'll be
clean and
quiet, and say Yessir

nosir.
I don't even
miss them, I
miss

browbeating them.
I don't know why
I'm saying this.
– Because it's true.

I don't know why
it's true. The
voice you have
put in my

head doesn't
take me over –
I don't
let it, like those

people." He
glared at
the bar.
"Of

course, you
know that . . .
The truth is,
I haven't been happy

since before she
left. One
day we
went to a rally.

A Christian was
running for governor.
He
promised total war

on crime.
That meant blacks.
'Insiders' meant Jews.
Some

groups he had
to use circumlocutions
about, others
not.

We preferred it
when he did — it
made us feel . . .
informed. I

knew he wouldn't
save people's
factory
jobs or

my drugstore;
the
point was to
make us

forget. There were a lot
of television crews, and
everyone
tried to get interviewed

so we could
insult you.
(But
when they did

interview us, we giggled.
Why.
Because we were saying
cruel, stupid

things we didn't
understand.
Because we
hated you, and

thought it showed.)
I
remember the sky
was cool and

cloudless. We
found a good
parking space;
Ann said

how nice the
kids looked.
I wasn't
thinking about these

things
then, I don't
want to
now. Please.

Please. I
know my own
thoughts were
stupid, but

I want them
back.
You're supposed to
care about the

needs of
ordinary
people, aren't you?
You're supposed to be

the kindly ones?"

21

Rather moved, I
started to respond,
then realized
I had to piss.

"Hold
that thought,"
I said.
On the

way back from
the men's room, I
stopped at
the bar, where

Ric
(a pseudonym) was wiping
glasses. "The john is filthy,"
I

said. "I
want it cleaned up
by the next time we're
here." The

Trial was
over for
the day, and,
while Ric apologized,

I watched the wrap-up.
Headquarters
allowed heroic
music for this

part: Nielsen,
the Fifth,
the
Helios Overture. A thoughtful

montage of ongoing
punishments, with
(today) an
emphasis on gender

crimes:
guys
transposed to women's
bodies, then hit on,

hit,
demeaned,
raped by
carefully prepared

androids. We exchanged
perps' and victims'
ages and races; we subjected
willing victims

(already breaking down) to a vast
HA HA HA
HA HA
— it was harsh

but effective. Then
class —
these broadcasts
always ended with

class. A twilight image
of executives
starting to shovel
toxic

waste. One
made a peculiar
gesture ("Did you see
that?"

I asked
Ric): the
wide-armed V-sign
of Richard Nixon, expressing

neither irony nor sincerity.

22

Late afternoon
light was spreading
intricate
cubofuturist

patterns across
the
stamped-tin
ceiling. In

that light, the
faces of
bar-sitters
radiated a

sense
(however
spurious) of promise.
At our

table, the squad —
Keith
too, without
affectation, and as intensely

as the others — was discussing Why
Bad Things Happen to
Good People;
that was

more or less
the topic. I
leaned my chair
dangerously against the

wall and
reflected.
My second appointment
was late, probably

a no-show;
certain consequences followed.
The others
moved on to

Hawking's
apocalypse. Renata:
"What do you
think, chief?

Will it happen?" She had
let down her
terminal coolness for
a moment,

Evan his hipness,
Keith his fear.
I
grinned: "I think we have

our hands full, making
bad things happen to
bad people."
Evan:

"Seriously."
— "I am serious," I
said. "That's
why I pulled

the switch on
X-day,
why I stay
in the field and avoid

deskwork. As for the
apocalypse:
I don't care
whether it comes, so much as

whether it's adequate."
Renata,
I think,
understood;

Evan pretended to;
Keith
again goggled at
blasphemy. I

sighed: "Let me tell you a
story.
The original god
still exists. He's

nice but
distant, in the sense of
very far away.
Once everything was

his;
what we call
Creation was
really an act

of theft. I
call this god — the
ineffective
benign one —

the Intellectual. He is also,
of course, yourself,
just as the
gurus and pseudotherapists

claim:
what else could
he be? Long
ago, however,

an inferior spirit
muscled
in and became
the Creator, the

Lord of Causality.
Sometimes
the true god
sends a

Messenger, an
activist,
to enter the
prison the

false god
set up, and liberate everyone.
Invariably,
however, this

person becomes confused,
forgets his
name, the procedures . . .
But

you want to hear
about the usurper
god.
The one

people worship." I
ordered another round,
assured Ric
it was the last. "God,

you see,
likes pain. He doesn't *think*
in our sense, or any meaningful sense —
he

feeds. This is
success for him;
thought for him
ended with

that initial act of
expropriation. Instead he
elaborates
pain, and is endlessly,

breathtakingly petty: toestubbings,
muggings after
torture . . . The
true god

fights him;
he can do little
but that little
is beauty,

reason, etc. Of
course, God
dissolves all attempts
at something other than

pain back
into pain. Work becomes labor.
Sex becomes AIDS. Oh, he's
a fucker . . . "

I
laughed, thought,
drank. "Are you following me?"
I yelled. Evan

grunted. Renata,
intently: "Yes."
— "He
more or less has

this world sewn up:
our
bodies, most of our
minds. The Intellectual

can do practically
nothing. After
you die,
however, you

will find yourself climbing
a
narrow,
apparently endless

ramp between
the galaxies —" "Wearing
what?" asked
Renata,

urgently. —
"What?" I asked,
nonplussed.
— *What will I be*

wearing when I
awaken?"
— "Christ, I
don't know," I

laughed. "Whatever
you want.
Full body armor.
Spikes.

A chemise."

23

"He will throw everything
he has at
you
[I went on], and

generally it's
enough:
you die
again — for

real this
time —
in unprecedented pain
(he stabs your

eyes and
genitals), wondering
(if
anything) *why the anticlimax?*

was it some sort of
summary . . . If
you're
strong in

hatred — if you have hated
all your life, but
are still
flexible, you'll transfer it

to whatever lies
at the end of the
ramp, and
advance

several
meters before he
gets you. Some
few of

us — unusually
great-souled ones — get
far enough to
make him

squeal; for he is
a bully, and easily
frightened.
One

day, however, someone who
knows the score
will appear on
that ramp.

He or
she will endure
the needles, acid
spray, intimate

insults;
will see through
the illusions, the
reassurances.

He will put
one foot ahead of
the other, denying
the pain. And as

the pain is
defeated, he
or
she will momentarily

quail at the surrounding
void and hard
stars, then decide
to defeat them

too. In a
space suddenly,
entirely outside
Creation, he

will understand his
purpose, his
representativeness:
he will know

himself as
anyone who ever
climbed any
length of that

ramp.
And from that space
he will draw out
a weapon. The

ramp will be
no longer endless;
at
the end

God sits
exhausted, a
cringing degenerate — weeping
as you

draw near. I say you
because it may be
you.
The hero may be

already on his way.
He has just started.
He is
always on the point of

arriving. And when you
arrive, you will
raise your
sword

(− liberals
dislike this part, but
they could surprise themselves)
and

slice
into that
mindless, gibbering
face

and
gut − Oh, how the
blood spurts (as Artaud
predicted) . . . You might also

take your
time,
smash his
face repeatedly into

the ramp, once
for every
victim of
gas, torture, arbitrary

death (or death itself,
for that matter), terminal
loneliness − for
lousy wasted

lives or even
your own
minor crap.
He was gigantic

but
diminishes in your hands. And all this
has no
psychological

repercussions; this isn't a
mind, a
person you're dealing with . . .
The

face is
turned
away, pouring
blood, yet as if

searching, too
late, for
an idea.
You'll know he's dead

when the stars go
out. Only the corpse
remains, then
that also

goes — the way
corpses go
here. And the ramp
stays, but even

that may go —
as if
you had forced him
to build it." — "Then what?"

asked Renata.
I
shrugged. I was about
two-thirds drunk, and

tired.
"That's up to you,
isn't it?
The point is,

it isn't up to
Stephen." In
their
silence, I

returned to
what I had been
thinking, and
glanced at

my watch.
A
washout, I thought.
Typical, I almost said.

"Let's go," I said.

24

Asleep that
night in our building
nearby, Renata
sensed

something; rolled to the floor,
gun out.
Nothing. She
checked the

hallway. — "What's wrong?"
Evan
emerged from
his room, laser pistol

also drawn. Keith's
room was empty,
neat.
"He took his Bible,"

she noticed. – "There's an
RNA monitor
attached to the Glove,"
said

Evan. "It can be used
as a tracer." The
armory was in
the basement; they

confronted the AI
guard, reset
the equipment.
Keith's

trail led past
the warehouses,
ruined
machine-shops and bars

of the neighborhood. The
half-sky
left by the
Wall was full

of stars;
the
Wall gave
its own murky

light. Five blocks from it,
they found where he had
vomited.
Two more blocks,

blood on a crumbling
curb. They
tried to gaze
ahead. "Unbelievable,"

gasped Evan.
Renata also fought
for air. — "Are there side streets —"
It hurt to

talk; her ears hurt.
— "No —
trace goes
right up —" They

inched back.
"There goes the fucking
Avengers of Wrong,"
she said.

Evan: "We'll find someone more
compatible."
— "Won't be the same."
— "We should've

helped him."
— "We
did," she growled.
"He was an asshole

with asshole pride and courage."
It was strange,
she thought,
being

back in
this neighborhood
at night
and fearing

nothing.
"Given the
time-displacement effect, he
could be anywhere,"

said Evan. "He
may be responsible for
capitalism. Or religion.
More likely he's

dead."
— "Or dead and
displaced,"
said Renata. "I've

always suspected that
history is somebody's
rotting corpse."
— "You sound like

the chief,"
said Evan. "I suppose
we should wake him."
They

did, which I regretted;
in
dreams, I had returned
to that moment of

the afternoon
when I walked
the second floor of
a building. Now the

old Marxist's
door remained closed, but
his neighbor's
opened. The light

outlined her body
under a thin robe,
accented
her hair,

unreadable
expression and clenched
fists, and I
started to ask her

what *she* wanted.

3

25

Hawking called
a few nights later.
He, also,
awakened me. "The

field won't
attract enough
particles,"
he announced. "You

mustn't blame yourself;
my
calculations were at fault." −
"Particles," I

said stupidly.
− "Yes,
they were the most
interesting aspect of

this project. O-
muons:
particles of Being
itself,

as it were. You
see it's impossible
even for me to
speak of them without

metaphor." − I:
"So
there won't be any
apocalypse."

He: "I'm afraid
not. At least, not the one
I imagined."
— "What about the

Anomaly?
What we have
so far?
Aidenn?" — "Oh,

that also goes. Without
concentration there's
dispersal, and
what we have is

dispersal."
I asked him when;
he said soon.
Weeks, months. A

month. The
tone, after the
flurry of apology, was
characteristically flat;

perhaps a hint
of sadness.
"What will you do?"
I

asked — slowly
thinking that suicide
wouldn't work.
"It depends," he said,

explaining the
obvious, "on the
time-displacement effect.
In most eras

I won't last long.
In our own
time and
space, there is a Chair

waiting for me."

26

That morning I
went on leave,
thereby effectively disbanding
the squad. We

met in
an empty room. (Our
barracks had been
speculative,

never-occupied offices;
my mind ran on
offices
that would now reacquire

us.) "Dispersal," said
Renata.
— "Not
noticeable," I said,

"before the end.
Which will be
instantaneous: the Wall simply
implodes. Until that

point, we may even
grow stronger." —
"I won't go back,"
she cried, then

half-laughed:
"Does that sound immature, or
what —" *"They'd* certainly
think so,"

said Evan, too
brightly. "'Maturity' being
the property of
people like my former . . .

firm. *We* were too weak,
too
childish to go on being
employees, consumers —" "Being

ugly," said Renata.
"That's what I can't
accept.
Ugly and stupid." She

paused. "I'll
keep the M-60 —"
I:
"You'll

return it to headquarters
when you report.
We can keep
sidearms." — "Sidearms should be

enough," muttered
Evan, "once we're
on the other
side and death

obtains."
He started to say
he couldn't be punished,
there was no law

for what he had done; but
Renata asked: "What about
the jeep?" — "I take that,"
I said. Where are you

going, they asked.
I told them.
Take us with you, they
begged. I

shook my head: "You're
needed.
Right up until the last
minute.

To heal and punish;
to
set an example.
To create,

if nothing else,
a memory. I'm needed too
but I'm on leave." — "I
won't go back,"

said
Renata, this time
quietly. Evan became
calm: "It's been fun,

anyway . . . " I
embraced them,
quoted
Trotsky: "In a good cause

there are no failures."

27

Then I drove
north and east.
A
peculiarity of

the O-muon
field was that
its strength was
proportional to

distance. I.e.:
the
farther from
the Wall, the less intervention

was needed, and we knew little
about those regions.
"Time is
probably

dilated there and
space somewhat –"
"Contracted?" – "Let's say
more coherent,"

said Stephen, the
one time
we discussed it. He was,
as usual, impatient:

he knew the math,
the landscape
didn't concern him. Now I drove,
AWOL, away from

the Wall.

28

Denver appeared, its
sky
smog-free, nourished by
truck-gardens

and
parks that had replaced
the office-parks.
Above its

towers, solar panels
gleamed and wheeled;
below them
flickered (like `

thoughts) the clean and noiseless
mag-levs.
On AM,
a woman of

the former local underclass described
her life. Without
edits or
music

or more than subtly
leading questions, the
soft voice was
unbearable; and when it finished

there would be another —
a
worker perhaps — and another.
I didn't stop

in Denver. It was still,
in some sense, Denver, and
the mountains
called. At an

insane but
perfectly safe
speed, I raced towards them – straining
my deathless

batteries. Light
etched
every crag and
tree, and the air

seemed to breathe
itself, becoming purer.
It was the wind
of the Revolution, the

mild sun of
the Revolution; no one now,
I
thought, would

ever again use
these metaphors. Yet
fall
had always been

my season. Other people
start to think and lust
in spring, but I
only when air

(like that Neizvestny sculpture
of the soul) pulls away
its gas-mask. And as I sped
towards the notional limit

of our
field, it seemed that fall
slowed towards
stillness within

contracted space, dilated time.

29

In the new settlements
(their
mission
reforestation), I planted trees,

checked pests,
tested
water, weighed trout.
I

spread gravel
for new trails, laid
cable for computers.
Otherwise

I hoed tomatoes,
gathered
herbs, aloes,
earths for

soap-making,
washed and mended
tough versatile
fabrics, tended

cows in
the fly-free
barn. I
tried

and failed
to cook. After
meals, I scrubbed pots,
sorted garbage,

composted.
Periodically, the
nightsoil collectors added
me to

their rota. In the nursery
I wiped asses,
boiled formulas,
rocked

insomniacs; in
school I taught
music appreciation.
I did chores

for pregnant comrades. Always
I was conscious of
the season, the
thin, slowly-recovering

forest,
the animals who live
no more effortlessly than
we do, some more alone,

some less. And always
I was conscious
of myself. It was not "we"
or

"one" who performed
as described, or
who sat
revising morality and ethics

around
bonfires; it was always
I,
and I who left —

pleading
fatigue — when
the others,
tired but exalted, discussed

the future . . .
I had said nothing.
Yet I knew
I had to leave.

First rumor would come,
then nightmarish impotence, then
doom.
Time, though

immensely slowed, was
still insufficiently slow
for me.
The

intensity of our field
approached infinity
higher in the
mountains, above

the narrowest
mud road.
At the
last camp, I

gave them
the jeep (they were grateful)
and my
gun (they appeared

bemused). Taking
only the radio, I climbed.
Night fell. The
way upward

led through snow,
thorns, a growing feeling
of pressure, sudden
noise,

bright light and pain.

30

Evenings before bedtime,
I
lay between
Daddy and Mommy,

feeling my energy
ooze into
them to be
stored; then

feeling myself lifted,
carried,
tucked in.
Mornings, I

didn't need them. Once
coordination and waste-control
were achieved, I tottered
through meadows,

our
garden, the approaches
to the forest;
one or both

parents (soon
"Vlad" and
"Mindy") came with me
or

watched on
their monitors. (Robots lurked
by trees or hovered,
their eyes

transmitting; we
talked, but
their only interest
was safety.)

Afternoons I sat
at my terminal. Soon I spent
mornings there too;
Vlad

and Mindy
urged me to play
outdoors, and came with me,
carrying

nets and
quirky floating balls.
(Evenings, variants of
golden

light – green, copper, russet –
entered the
house. I
ran then,

yelled etc. – frantic to enter
that golden light.)
My monitor
was flat for print and graphics,

otherwise a
sphere. The
animals it showed
were, at first, animals

outside: otters and birds
(wolves and bears
in the forest), then
distant, extinct, or

on other worlds. By the time
I could read their
names, I was interested
only in math:

Mindy was
a mathematician.
Basics
bored her, but Vlad made

them fun. When I reached calculus,
her
slow delighted
smile rewarded

me. ("I love you,
you know, even without
calculus," she said,
but I wanted

her smile).
Then
math was
no longer interesting:

I was spending
more time with
Vlad and
his interests — some of which,

amazingly, the computer
knew nothing of:
building
toys,

bowls, cabinets from
precious wood
("All wood is precious,"
he said) in

his sweet-smelling,
sawdust-coated
shed.
He could do anything:

had been a spacer;
an
engineer both on
and off earth; had

worked,
like many former spacers, undersea —
but what he loved,
besides me and Mindy,

was carpentry . . . When I grew bored,
he was hurt.
(Mindy, I
think, was

relieved when I
dropped math.
So
there was still pain

apparently, character-building etc.)
When I
wasn't studying, or
playing with

other children, I
began, now, to wander
downhill,
over the clearings,

along the paths of
the nearer woods, to the houses
of other grownups.
Khushwant

was a painter
and
doctor. Elena "served
necessary infrastructural functions"

(as she put it) systemwide
from her
terminal;
otherwise gardened,

listened to
music, read.
She lived alone.
Jin, a fantastic

cook and
architect, lived
with Khushwant.
My favorite was Carl,

a historian.
(He didn't do
anything else, I
thought.) Jin had

designed his house;
Vlad had built
shelves and cupboards.
Khushwant painted

murals on
his second floor;
then they quarreled;
then made up when

(I
learned) Carl
renounced Jin. — His house was
darker than ours,

with red-brown surfaces
too
spare for
dust

(except for the books
and crystals everywhere),
then a lit area
around his

big decayed chair,
strangely-patterned
rug, and pipe-rack.
Carl

smoked. "Do I thereby
defy or obey convention?"
was an
early problem

he set me.
(It was a paradox:
he was *supposed* to be
unconventional.) His

voice was
gruff: "This is a
'child village.'"
We discussed what

that meant. Vlad
and Amanda,
Khushwant and Jin,
thirty or

forty such couples "are
tested, found
suitable,
trained, and

agree to stay together — if
possible — till
the kids (no more than two)
are sixteen.

That, as you know,
is when you leave. If
births are
spaced, the contract

is correspondingly lengthened." He
waited while
I considered
what all this implied about

me.
I had known it, more or
less, and wasn't
frightened. "If they accept

the rules, one or
both parents keep
the house.
Some stay on

afterwards, because they like the
life, and
can help.
Local examples are me

and Elena.
My son is named
Rudi." He
began to describe

the unregulated
prerevolutionary system, which resulted in
"genetic diversity, but also in
billions and billions of people

who knew themselves, at
best, to be meaningless . . . " I
said, however,
I knew enough

about that for
now;
I wanted to hear
about space.

(When I asked Vlad
about space, his
eyes grew distant
and wistful;

Carl's became stern.) "It's
impossible to judge,"
he murmured,
mostly to

himself.
"It has become
coterminous with experience.
(Look up 'coterminous.')

The good part is: we
no longer run
the risk of being destroyed, we're on
too many worlds.

The bad —" But I forget
what he said, or was
about to say;
Tholi

came in, a
girl from the
balloon houses
near village center. Her

current interest was
racism, and
we talked about that . . .
As

she and I
left, a flight of geese
was just organizing
itself over

the far slope. They
dipped and wheeled, extended
their necks,
labored

forward. For a while
I lost myself
in them, and in
the sounds of

our
valley, which people of
the crowded past
would have thought silent.

Then I wondered
if she was bored. She
was humming.
"Why do they need a

leader?" she asked. —
"I don't know if
the lead goose *is*
a leader,"

I said
(proud of myself;
girls are supposed to be
smarter). She

then, in
the same tone: "Would you have
oppressed me because I'm
black?"

"I don't know,"
I said. "We're not
living back then.
I don't think so." — She seemed

mistrustful, and I felt
a guilt and
helplessness that were
not mine . . . they made me angry,

but I thought,
It isn't real
anger.
Silently we continued

towards the stores.
Gradually we
began to discuss
adults we liked. She was

spending time with Colin
(like
Elena, primarily a reader
and listener)

and
Ti-lei, who
had failed to start a theatre group.
(People saw

the need, but only abstractly).
"But the main reason
is Arthur. Their son."
— "Main reason for

what?" — "Main reason I
hang out there," she
giggled;
gazed at me, and

ran off. I realized
something I knew about
was starting.
I

reacted, I think,
like any
boy of
that village: repressing the knowledge,

yet knowing I
was repressing it, and
without
fear. — I wondered where

to sleep that night.
Recently I'd stayed
at Carl's.
I liked

arranging, then
browsing (until
one or
two A.M.) a pile of books

on the bedside table
in the
neat brown room
that had been Rudi's.

(And in the mornings:
"No
breakfast for you
till you put those back!" — then

vast breakfasts.)
The smell of
his pipe permeated and
shaped me,

like,
elsewhere, that of Jin's
enticing vegetable stews,
sweet-and-sour

fish, Khushwant's paints,
and at home
the smell of wood . . . In my
earlier years, when

I became lonely
in the middle of the
night, or Vlad or Mindy
suddenly

missed me, a robot,
summoned, would
carry me — blanketed,
crying, then sleeping —

through the night,
so that I woke
in my own bed. (There was a large,
humorous folklore around such

adventures,
but for me
they were already past.) More
recently I had slept

in great heaps of
kids —
at Franzo's house
and Rahman's

and Tholi's, but not for
a while: I liked
to talk, I liked the
girls' bawdy wit

but
sex play palled
short of puberty . . . Games
palled. (One was expected

vaguely to despise sports, but
play anyway.) Only
solitude had charm,
my computer and

books, a few
friends
and adults. "You're waiting for puberty
the way people at

prerevolutionary resorts waited
for the season," said
Elena.
— "Not just me,"

I said. She laughed:
"I meant 'you'
collectively." She had
the same bluff

objectivity I liked
in Carl
and a few others, and
(I now realized)

in myself . . . "Rather like your mother,"
she said. (It was the night
after I saw the
geese, and

I was describing,
stumblingly,
my character.) — I
agreed. Elena,

concerned: "You don't think
she doesn't love you —"
I: "I know she loves me . . .
She's

unsentimental." — Elena:
"Some people confuse them."
I, pursuing the
insight: "I have this other

side, this . . . "
"Find a word,"
said Elena
(the way they

all did).
"Take your time, but
always find a word." — "This
dreaminess.

Sometimes I lose myself,
for hours, contemplating
things. I
get that from Vlad.

From
my father."
She: "How do you
feel about it?"

I: "I like it." —
"Good," she said, but
we were interrupted
by her terminal.

A factory
somewhere in the
depopulated zones was
bottlenecked.

The code,
rapid and arcane, filled
the screen; when it let up,
she explained. First

she had to locate
the factory. (Bangladesh,
the Shoreline Extension.)
Then the problem. —

Not in the building
or at the port . . .
It turned out
a bridge was gone, and

circuits in a
survey sked; hence the pileup
of rare ores, down from the lunar
mines. It's important

(Khushwant had
said) to
notice — artist or otherwise! —
what you ignore; to become interested

in what bores you. Other
times at Elena's,
all I had noticed
was her bric-a-brac, the

plants from
several
worlds, her pillows and games,
comfortable

disorder, the
music she made me
listen to for
hours (explaining how

it worked), and,
increasingly,
her body.
Her "job" (she used

the old word) had been
a distraction.
Now, suddenly, I admired
her reach,

her
role in things
one actually used. I too wanted
(did not have

the words immediately, but
soon)
to have an effect. To
be noticed.

To give.
— Vlad was pleased;
Carl mourned
("for now, at least")

a budding historian.
Khushwant said,
"Well, you weren't an artist
anyway"; Tholi said:

"Troubleshooting is
neat!" After three months, with
Elena on
override, I routed

firefighting robots
to a flier-repair
plant whose systems
had failed. After six months

she
said she would trust me
with machinery in
inhabited zones; when I left

the village, I could seek
a certificate.
— But by now,
much had changed.

The far woods,
the
whole length of
our river

were open to
my age-group. We
took survival training and
set out, only

one guardian
drifting above
our rafts.
We

stopped at
other
settlements,
compared

interests, checked out
girls, boys, and
cooking, but
did not bring

anyone from those villages
aboard: this was *our* trip;
they would take
their own. The

third night we camped
on a broad beach under
an overhang.
(People, we

knew, had
lived here once;
we thought about them.)
We

put up a field
against ticks, snakes, and
fleas. We
swam,

cooked, ate,
washed dishes, then sat
around a fire drinking
decaf. – "I haven't seen you at

Carl's," said Franzo.
– I: "I got interested
in engineering.
Elena from

north valley supervises
twenty factories, ground
and orbital.
I've been studying

with her this year." — He,
mildly: "But
you spent years with
Carl.

He had great hopes
for you. Insofar as I
too have
committed myself, I can't help but feel

disappointed."
— "I
haven't renounced history,"
I said. "It means a lot,

still, that I can
measure an
evening like this against
the past and know

how impossible
it would have been.
I'll never give up
that perspective.

But I have nothing
to add to it." — "Why 'impossible'?"
asked Rahman
(famously

interested
only in
biology).
I was relieved,

being able to shift
into describing those obscure institutions —
"entertainment,"
"school,"

"style" etc. — on which
our
brothers and
sisters of the

past had shattered.
And Adni, Arthur's
sister, raised
(predictably) the point

that capitalism had underlain
these: "Adults didn't
respect themselves except as
property; how could

we respect ourselves?"
— "Some of the
music was fun, though,"
said someone.

"Overtly sexual."
We
sat grown quiet
at the term sex.

Kids
vanished by twos and
threes into
the darkness. Now I

had to bear
the consequences of
my loner act
of the past year:

Tholi
was off with Arthur, and
I hadn't attracted
anyone else. Aimlessly I

circled the
campfire, where
Enver (a late
developer, or

determined, for some reason,
to be cool) softly
played
guitar. "Someone might feel

like switching, later. Or
group action,"
he said.
(The tone, I realized,

was consoling.) I:
"You counting on that?" –
He shrugged. I sat
beside him and we talked

about the forthcoming
Leavetaking Day,
the last before
our own. A ritual

of people who had
outgrown
ritual, it had
a junior component: "What have you

prepared?" I asked.
For
answer he played
a breathtaking riff. – "You?" –

"A wood sculpture . . .
I
have it under wraps
in the studios.

I was pissed at
Khushwant for saying
I'd given up art . . .
I also thought

I'd tape my
factory interventions, but
technical surveys require
too much voice-over." — "That's a weakness

of the format," agreed
Enver.
"It also discourages
group projects. I'm

going into education; I'll reform it!"
So we
chatted, sometimes
laughing at the

noises in
the woods. When
he nodded off, I
walked to

the water's edge.
The
river, passing, gathered
glints of

firelight. Overhead,
the robot
occluded some stars;
watching others (— had

the Pole drifted?
How far ahead
was I?), I
had several insights.

One involved
work: what I would
study next year in
the city;

what I would do.
Another
related to
egregious moans and

screams beyond
the fire.
I have time,
I thought; but

what I was mostly
imagining was
Elena — standing across
the Green at

Leavetaking:
kids who were leaving
on one side,
my cohort opposite;

she in the crowd
of parents and younger
kids; I catching her eye,
she

mine . . . Why was she
more attractive than
girls my age,
I wondered, feeling

madly
horny and interestingly
perverse. "What do you think
you're doing?"

asked Stephen.
When I
was silent, he
said "It

took us quite a while
to find you." —
I: "You could have fucking
waited till I

got laid."

31

And having said
that, I
jerkily paced
the riverbank — deaf to

irony, recriminations,
pleas,
appeals to
(bourgeois or revolutionary)

virtue, false
hints that our field
might not disintegrate —
until Hawking and

other voices from
headquarters
left me alone,
and

Aidenn became
my world again.
And shortly thereafter,
what I had imagined

occurred:
I
lay beside Elena,
wondering

at her sumptuous breasts,
her
scent, her
amused benign

smile, and
what felt like
a vast new
aura around my life.

I was
suddenly dreadfully
inarticulate but didn't care.
The

wind whipped
branches against
her window
and the red leaves

blew by. "You learn quickly,
in
this as in other fields,"
she said

and spoke my name
with an unprecedented,
tender
stress. The

next year was
easy,
though I'm afraid
I read little. Then

I too stood
on the concrete strip,
the morning after
Leavetaking,

reluctantly
remembering the
night. *Some appear to remember,
others struggle*

*to remember; most
cry*
wrote a poet
about parents on

that night.
Mindy
had cried.
Adults, by

custom, were not present
on the tarmac,
but I didn't
turn around

till the bus landed.
(Carl alone had
broken the taboo;
we

waved.) I went to Saskatchewan.
It had another
name. But
with the change (and

then the
troubled changing back)
of climate, the migration
of peoples

and then of
survivors, the cities had
absorbed the names
of regions. This one

housed precious
relics: a Braque gueridon.
A
Klee. It had a plaza —

Revolution Square — around which
all life
centered, and where,
long

ago, people had hanged
the last arbitrageur.
It had a Museum
of the Revolution, and a

Museum of Science and Art. —
I found a room
in the "Clouds." Back in
the village, adults had said

their first night in
that crowded,
off-the-ground environment had
decided them

someday to live
entirely surrounded by trees.
I didn't
feel that way. The

lights of
passing
fliers swept
my bare walls. Strangers

returning from some party
laughed on the catwalk.
I
gazed at

my terminal,
my
still-empty,
built-in

shelves, and
thought of the operation
(just
perfected) that

made the entire Net
available to the brain. No
more terminals or
archaic

keyboards; one's memory
accessed all culture, whose
words,
sounds, images an

eyeblink could dispel.
And one could
transmit . . .
The usual controversy

about *control* filled
the news. But
no one on
this planet now sought

control, and "it was our duty
to keep it that way"
etc. — I approved,
but without interest.

The
room, the city still
absorbed me: I
felt I was

new-born, and born whole,
ready . . . that
Vlad,
Mindy and the

rest were all
the benign nothingness
before my birth.
— My walls filled up

with holograms of
art from
the Square;
then, as I

befriended artists, originals.
I traded
books for crystals,
crystals for books. I

hung out, till
all hours, in the cafes;
found
groups containing

graduates of
my village, then other groups. What our
ancestors at
their warmest felt

for "family"
occurred to one,
here, during
these all-night sessions

of posturing, boasting,
learning.
I
made friends.

Some became
lovers.
My small room
began to acquire

traces of other lives. — Otherwise
I walked,
hour after hour, beside
our little

reclaimed
river, watching
grass and leaves,
water eddying

around rocks,
people on
the banks, vast
amorphous starships rising

slowly and
silently from
the spaceport; and thought,
pleaded, *not*

yet not yet not yet . . .
After a month
I began courses.
Years passed.

I took all
the courses.
There was no external
discipline at first, no one

to demand
pushups and antigrav workouts
or
math

(I could do
the math), languages,
the O-muon
drive, xenobiology,

xenosociology. Only,
when one showed up
in the great hall
at the spaceport, one

was ready.
Few
showed up.
My

parents came, older,
still together,
proud.
Carl came.

There were people
in serviceable uniforms.
There was a step
forward,

an oath,
hors-d'oeuvres.
Eventually Carl and I
talked. The Academy

looked out over
Saskatchewan. Trees moved
in the chill,
quick-shifting wind.

In fall colors
they resembled
thousands of tiny fruits:
plum

purples,
apple reds, pear
golds.
"I loved it here,"

I said.
— "The town?" —
I nodded.
"What scared you,

Carl, years
ago, when we first
talked about space?" —
He shrugged:

"Freedom, I suppose . . . We've
learned,
somewhat, how to handle
freedom, but

old lessons are easy
to forget.
Some people *are*
forgetting, out there.

I wasn't thinking
of you, then . . .
Now I have
something else to fear." I

wanted to tell him
I'd be OK, but it
sounded inane.
"I've kept up

my prerevolutionary studies,"
I stammered.
"There was a poet,
Communist-era,

Jarrell —" Carl:
"I know Jarrell."
— "'*Who*
fights for his own life

loses, loses; I have struck
for my world
and am free ... '"
Quoting, I thought

I'm being pretentious —
I haven't fought for
anything ...
I would, though.

My real training —
years
of it — would only begin
now.

I regretted
(though not
severely) having no one
in particular to leave.

Maybe I'd find her
out there
among the stars (as a popular song
had it. Songs were plentiful

and unrecorded).
Meanwhile
I would find
other friends. — My

fantasies that day
were, I think,
pardonable,
given my youth.

I
should have been imagining
trade talks,
terraforming, first

contacts etc. but
I wasn't.
My
ship — torn from

its peaceful scientific pursuits —
had to square off
against unreasonable, even
psychotic aliens, who

would not accept us
as minds. Or against
humans,
spilled forth

long ago and forgotten,
who had regressed or
adhered to
old ways:

marching;
torture. I
was at the controls —
still utterly

green, but it didn't matter:
all I had to
do
(all I

could do) was —
with our
last power, and
systems failing — pursue

the enemy
(our last
enemy) into his
gravity-well, coolly

aiming our last
missiles, thinking
At
least the wasted

years are not
behind me, and
rallying
(with my mind)

our immense fleet.

32

And yet
I was denied
my own death:
the Wall

collapsed at that moment. —
There was pain,
but
worse was the sense

of being disarmed, of having
no sure aim or
target.
Because I cannot

shake that sense, it doesn't matter
where — after
the noise,
the swiftly-returning

stench (you're unaware of it) —
I wound up;
whether I shrink
from spears or guns;

whether I see
on torchlit gibbets,
futile
panels, my fellow plotters

or in lonely rooms
only imagine them.
The worst is
images of victors

that come
over whatever medium. And I would name them,
but such names
seem always old.

I can describe them: fat or thin,
grey or
flushed, they have faces that,
like condoms, repel

blame. I can accuse them —
henchmen,
epigones of
death and its lord,

they will hunt every
one of us
down.
(Critique finds this point

difficult.) All
death is
death on their terms: a
death *we* chose

would be none, would be freedom.
I saw this,
fought,
lost, and the Wall fell.

It was summer.